THE GLORIE ST

Gym Glorie's ...-out

ISHMAEL

Susanna whites book

Susanna white

Phoenix

Very early in the morning in Glorieland, when the sun is considering whether it wants to come out or not, and the birds are getting their voices in tune ready for singing, all that can be heard from the little Glorie houses is the sound of gentle snoring.

From all the houses except one, that is. Right at the end of Joyful Lane, if you listen carefully, you will hear some strange huffing and puffing sounds coming from within. Gym Glorie is doing some press-ups as part of his daily work-out.

Gym Glorie is the fittest, healthiest, strongest, and one of the best-looking Glories in Glorieland. He has the best teeth, because he eats all the right foods; he is the perfect weight, because he doesn't eat too much of the right foods; and his springs have so much bounce that when he bounces up and down praising God, he gets so high that he can see in upstairs windows (though of course he doesn't look).

One morning, when Gym had finished his press-ups, he decided to go for a five-mile bounce before breakfast. Of course breakfast for Gym was not bacon and eggs, with toast and butter. Absolutely not. Breakfast was fruit juice with no additives, some muesli with no sugar, tea with no milk, and an apple.

Dawn was just dawning when Gym opened his front door and set off. It was rather chilly, for the sun still hadn't made up its mind, but the air was refreshing, and Gym felt almost as good as he looked.

After he had bounced a couple of miles into the countryside, he noticed a heap of black clothes lying by the path. Being just a little bit nosy, he stopped and went over to take a look at it. To his amazement it looked like it was breathing. 'Wow!' thought Gym, 'I've never seen living clothes before.' Gym was strong and was sure that there was nothing to be afraid of, so he prodded the black rags with the end of his spring.

'Ouch!' screamed the clothes. Poor old Gym was so surprised that he lost his balance and fell flat on his back.

Out of the old clothes appeared a head, a Miserie head. 'Oi! What's your game?' shouted the angry Miserie. 'Can't anyone get any peace around here, without being disturbed by some hyper-active Glorie?'

Gym sprang to his feet and apologised. 'I'm sorry,' he said, and tried to explain: 'I just thought you were some old clothes dumped by the path.'

Now the Miserie stood up, ready to give Gym a real mouthful. But then he noticed how fit and strong Gym looked—and changed his mind. He didn't fancy an argument with this guy, even if he was a Glorie.

You see, Miseries hate Glories. Glories were always so nice and good, and worst of all they kept going on about God. The Miseries' aim in life was to make the most of any opportunity to pull Glories down, and eventually get rid of them altogether.

'My name's Maverick,' said the Miserie. 'But you can call me Mav.'

'Oh hi, Mav, I'm Gym,' said Gym.

'You look like a Glorie who knows how to look after himself,' said Mav with a touch of envy, and just then a nasty idea crossed his wicked mind and an evil grin appeared on his face.

'I suppose all Glories are as fit and active as you, with a physique like yours?' asked Mav, knowing full well they weren't.

'Well no, actually they aren't,' replied Gym, a little embarrassed.

'Well, don't you think that you should make them follow your example? I mean they would all be even happier, *and* better looking, if they were like *you*, wouldn't they?' continued Mav. 'Far be it from me to criticise,' he criticised, 'but some of them are in a bit of a state, aren't they?'

'I suppose most Glories are in poor condition,' said Gym thoughtfully. 'I've always left them just to get on and be themselves. But I think you're right—I need to tell them to shape up a bit.'

With this, Gym thanked Mav for his advice, and Mav just smiled and said, 'You're welcome,' thrilled to know that the advice he had given would cause trouble.

As Gym bounced back into Glorieland, the sun had decided to shine and the birds were singing their favourite Glorie song. Even the Glories had come to life and started to bounce about.

Jane Glorie was just collecting the milk from her doorstep when Gym bounced up to her and shouted, 'Morning, Jane. You know, you're much too skinny—you need to eat more healthy food like I do!' Jane burst into tears. She didn't like to be called skinny, especially first thing in the morning.

Timmy Glorie was rather tubby. He was bouncing down the road, taking his dog Woofles for walkies.

'Hi Timmy!' shouted Gym. 'You know, you're much too fat—you should eat less, then you could be slim like me!' Timmy looked down at his feet, and felt tears welling up as his lip began to quiver. He hated to be called fat, especially in front of Woofles.

Grandpa Glorie was sitting on a rocking chair in his porchway, reading his Glorie comic.

'Morning Grandpa!' shouted Gym. 'You know, it's lazy just sitting in a chair all day; you should be out for a morning bounce, then you would be as fit as I am!' Grandpa suddenly felt guilty and started to fidget—he loved to spend the morning reading his comic.

Throughout that day Gym upset everyone he met by saying they should all be like him.

Something had to be done.

Timmy Glorie had now recovered from being called fat. Seeing the hurt that Gym was causing, he decided to go and visit him. Determined to stop him, he and Woofles bounced up to his house.

As Timmy approached the house he heard a strange groaning sound coming from inside. He opened the front door, and peered round. Inside he saw a far-from-fit, far-from-strong and far-from-healthy Gym lying flat on the floor.

'What's up, Gym?' asked Timmy, bouncing over to him and looking very concerned. 'Ooooh,' groaned Gym, 'I've overdone it. My head aches, by back aches, and I even think I've pulled a muscle in my spring.'

Suddenly forgetting why he had come, Timmy prayed that God would make Gym better, and then tucked him up in his bed, suggesting that a rest not a work-out was what he needed.

In no time at all news spread about poor Gym, and soon his house was as busy as a railway station in the rush hour. It was full of Glories who brought him get-well cards and beautiful flowers. Timmy even gave him a box of chocolates, secretly thinking that he may refuse them—but he didn't!

Gym felt very guilty as he looked at all his friends. 'I'm sorry,' he said to them, 'God does not want you all to be like me—he wants you to be yourselves. He's not so much interested in the shape and size we are as whether or not we love him.' All the Glories surrounding his bed smiled and agreed.

Then as Gym began to doze off, they all bounced out of his house as quietly as possible.

On her way out, Jane decided that she would try eating a little more—it certainly would do no harm.

As Grandpa Glorie left, he decided to get a bit of exercise and to go for a short bounce—his rocking chair and comic would be there to look forward to when he got back.

As Timmy left he decided that, as Gym had kept the chocolates ... he would buy a bag of chips on his way home.